# DINO-HOCKEY

## LISA WHEELER

### ILLUSTRATIONS BY BARRY GOTT

CAROLRHODA BOOKS · MINNEAPOLIS · NEW YORK

For Matt, Bobbie, Tyler, and Evan
Harget with love from Aunt Lisa
—L.W.

For Rose
—B.G.

TO ICE ➤

Text copyright © 2007 by Lisa Wheeler
Illustrations copyright © 2007 by Barry Gott
This edition published for Monarch Books of Canada Limited in 2009

Carolrhoda Books
A division of Lerner Publishing Group, Inc.
241 First Avenue North
Minneapolis, MN 55401 U.S.A.

Website address: www.lernerbooks.com

ISBN 978-0-7613-4948-8

Manufactured in the United States of America
3 - DP - 10/1/11

The game begins at half past six,
when dinos grab their hockey sticks.

They play to win on icy floors—
**MEAT-EATERS** vs. **VEGGIESAURS!**

As their coaches shout advice,
red and green teams take the ice.

Socks and jerseys keep them warm—
cold-blooded beasts in uniform.

MEAT-EATERS—RED TEAM

T. REX—CENTER

TROODON—GOALIE

PTERODACTYL TWINS—WINGERS

ALLOSAURUS—DEFENSEMAN

RAPTOR—DEFENSEMAN

VEGGIESAURS—GREEN TEAM

TRICERATOPS—CENTER

ANKYLOSAURUS—GOALIE

DIPLODOCUS—WINGER

APATOSAURUS—WINGER

IGUANODON—DEFENSEMAN

STEGOSAURUS—DEFENSEMAN

Safety pads protect their bones.
Some have helmets of their own.

It's **T. Rex** and **Triceratops**.

The two face off. The game puck drops.

Then dinos battle for control.

Who'll be first to score a goal?

**Veggiesaurs** have got the puck!
**Stego** licks his stick for luck.

**Tricera** slips. He spins. He reels!
Watch out—check! And **Raptor** steals!

**Raptor** passes to **T. Rex**.

The goalie waits for what comes next.

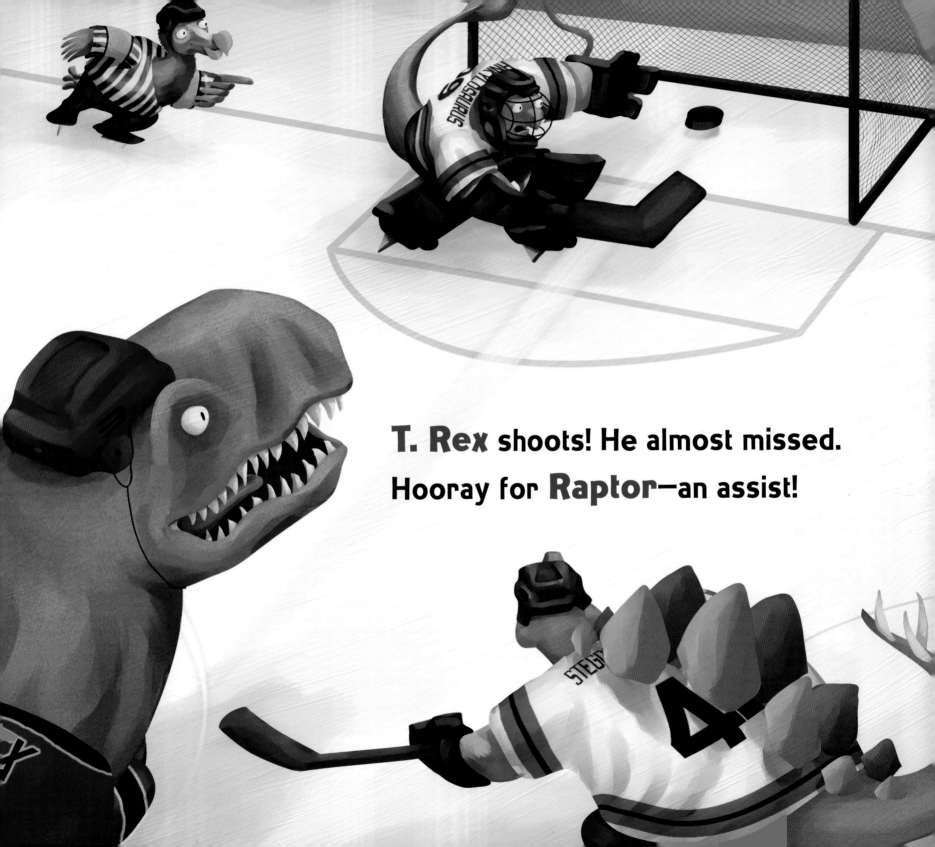

**T. Rex** shoots! He almost missed.
Hooray for **Raptor**—an assist!

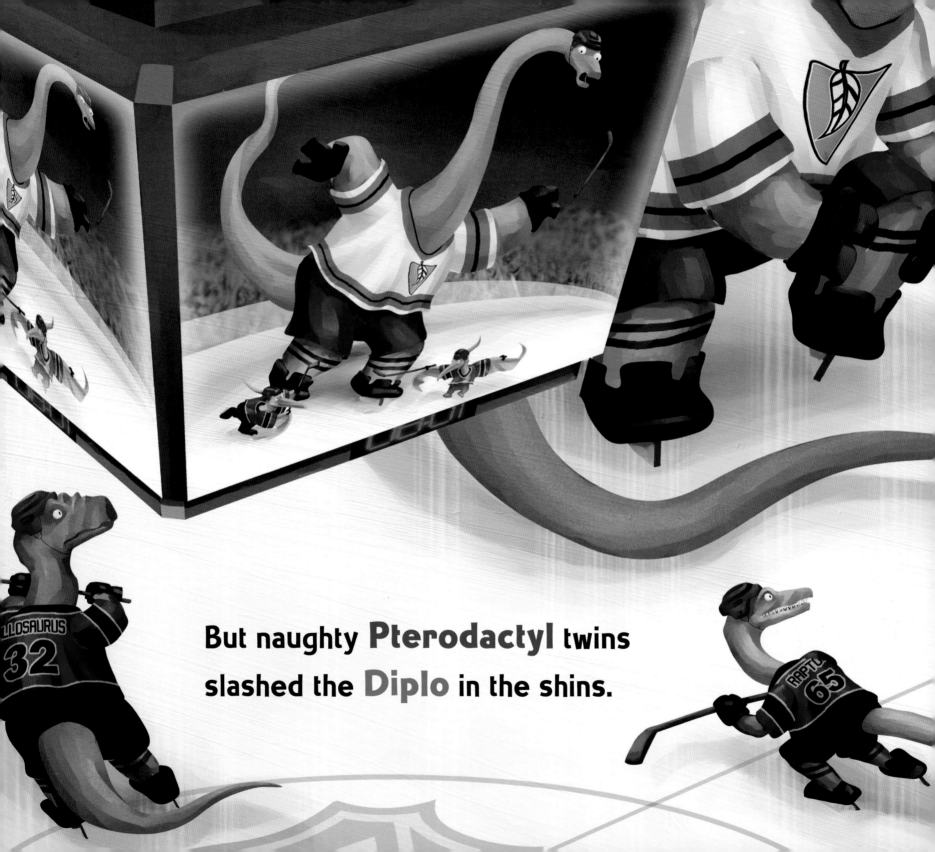

But naughty **Pterodactyl** twins slashed the **Diplo** in the shins.

Dodo is the referee.

The red team has a penalty!

The lines are drawn up in the stands, split by **Meat** and **Veggie** fans.

The twins fly by on hockey skates.
**Apatosaurus** hesitates.

**T. Rex's** pass is sure and quick,
received by **Raptor's** hockey stick.

**Raptor** doesn't miss a beat.
Shoots the puck at **Ankylo's** feet.

**Ankylosaurus** makes a save!
Excited sports fans do the wave.

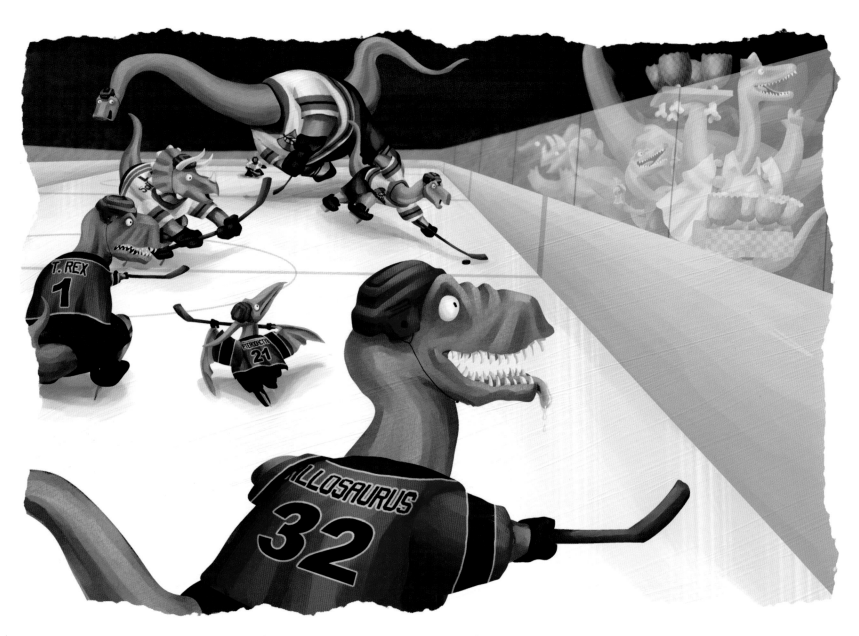

**Another face off. Veggies rule! Allosaurus starts to drool.**

Tries to check, but she's too slow.
The toothy fans shout, **"Go! Go! Go!"**

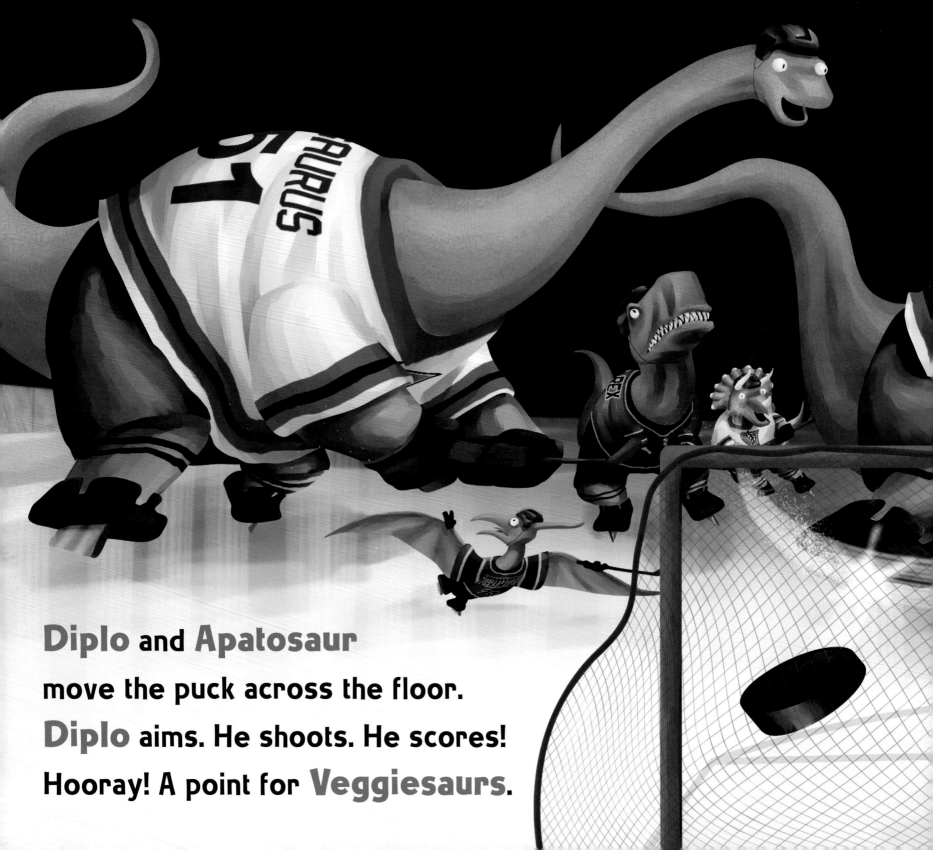

**Diplo** and **Apatosaur** move the puck across the floor. **Diplo** aims. He shoots. He scores! Hooray! A point for **Veggiesaurs**.

The score is tied now, 1 to 1.
The winner could be anyone.

The centers face off, nose to nose.

The puck is dropped between their toes.

**Tricera** sweeps. He gains control.
The **Veggiesaurs** are on a roll!

**Iguano** tries to clear the way
as **Veggies** keep the puck in play.

**Stego's** checked against the boards.
Oh no! It's dueling dinosaurs!

The two defensemen start to fight.
No fair! That **Raptor** tried to bite!

That's no way to win the cup!
The ref skates in to break things up.

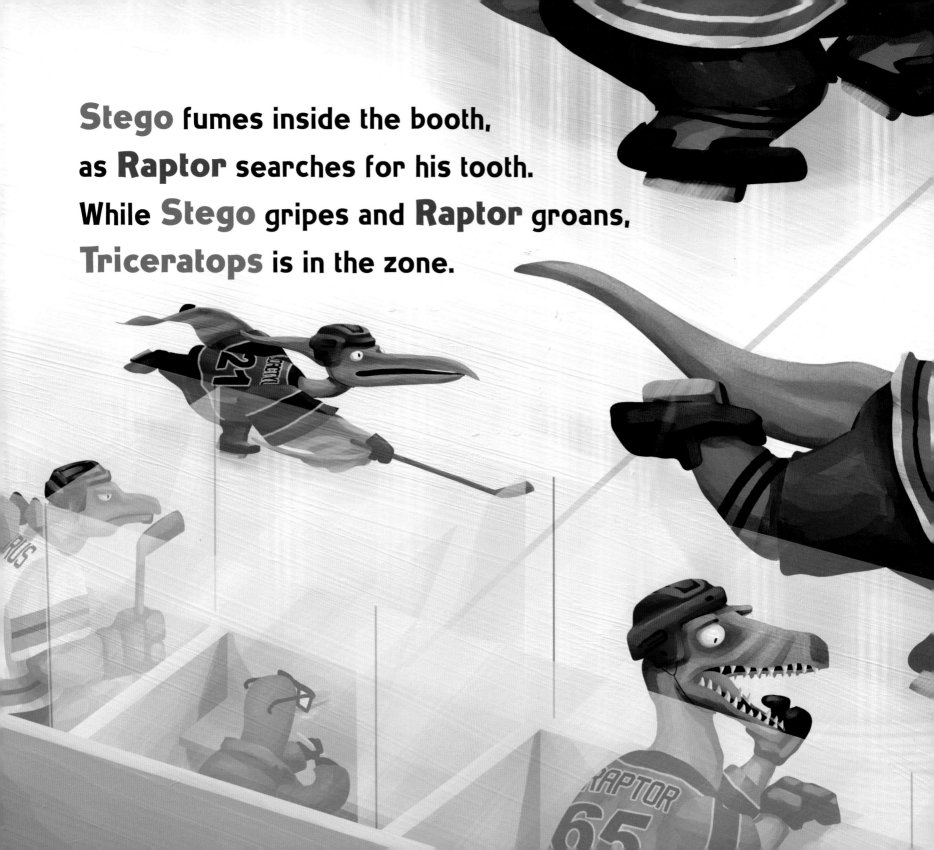

Stego fumes inside the booth,
as Raptor searches for his tooth.
While Stego gripes and Raptor groans,
Triceratops is in the zone.

He knows the game's not over yet—
a slap shot!—headed for the net.

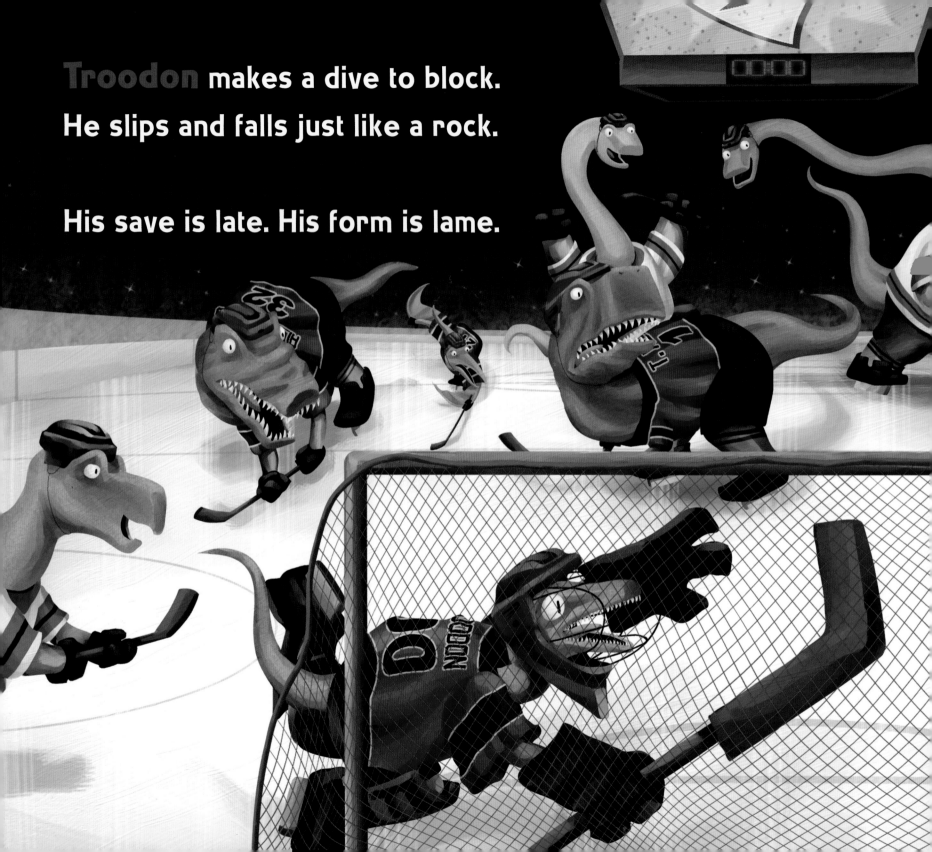

Troodon makes a dive to block.
He slips and falls just like a rock.

His save is late. His form is lame.

The fans of Veggies start to roar.
They've never won the cup before!

Fans grab the players—lift them up.
Tricera holds the winning cup.

As cameras flash,
the **Veggies** cheer.
The season's over
for the year.

But never fear . . .